Llama Llama Red Pyjama

written and illustrated by

Anna Dewdney

Hodder Children's Books

LLAMA LLAMA RED PYJAMA

Copyright © Anna Dewdney 2005
First published in 2005 by Viking, a division of Penguin Young Readers Group, USA
First published in the UK in 2012 by Hodder Children's Books,
338 Euston Road, London, NW1 3BH
Hodder Children's Books Australia, Level 17/207 Kent Street, Sydney, NSW 2000

A catalogue record of this book is available from the British Library.

ISBN 978 1 444 91087 2
10 9 8 7 6 5 4 3 2 1

Printed in China

Hodder Children's Books is a division of Hachette Children's Books.
An Hachette UK Company.
www.hachette.co.uk

For my own little llamas,

with thanks to Tracy, Denise and Deborah.

Llama llama
red pyjama
reads a story
with his mama.

Mama kisses
baby's hair.
Mama Llama
goes downstairs.

Llama llama red pyjama
feels alone without his mama.

Baby Llama wants a drink.

Mama's at
the kitchen sink.

Llama llama
red pyjama
calls down to
his llama mama.

Mama says
she'll be up soon.

Baby Llama hums a tune.

Llama llama
red pyjama
waiting waiting
for his mama.

Mama isn't coming yet.
Baby Llama
starts to fret.

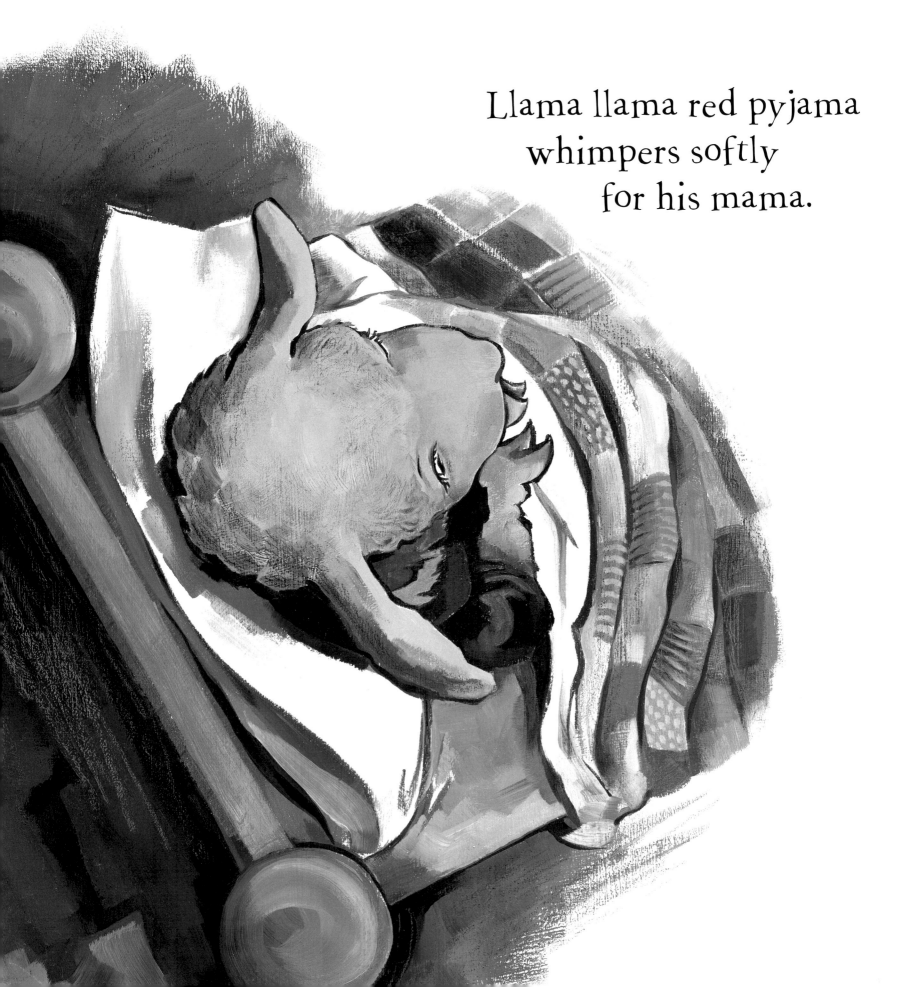

Llama llama red pyjama
whimpers softly
for his mama.

Mama Llama
hears the phone.

Baby Llama
starts to moan...

Llama llama
red pyjama
listens, quiet,
for his mama.

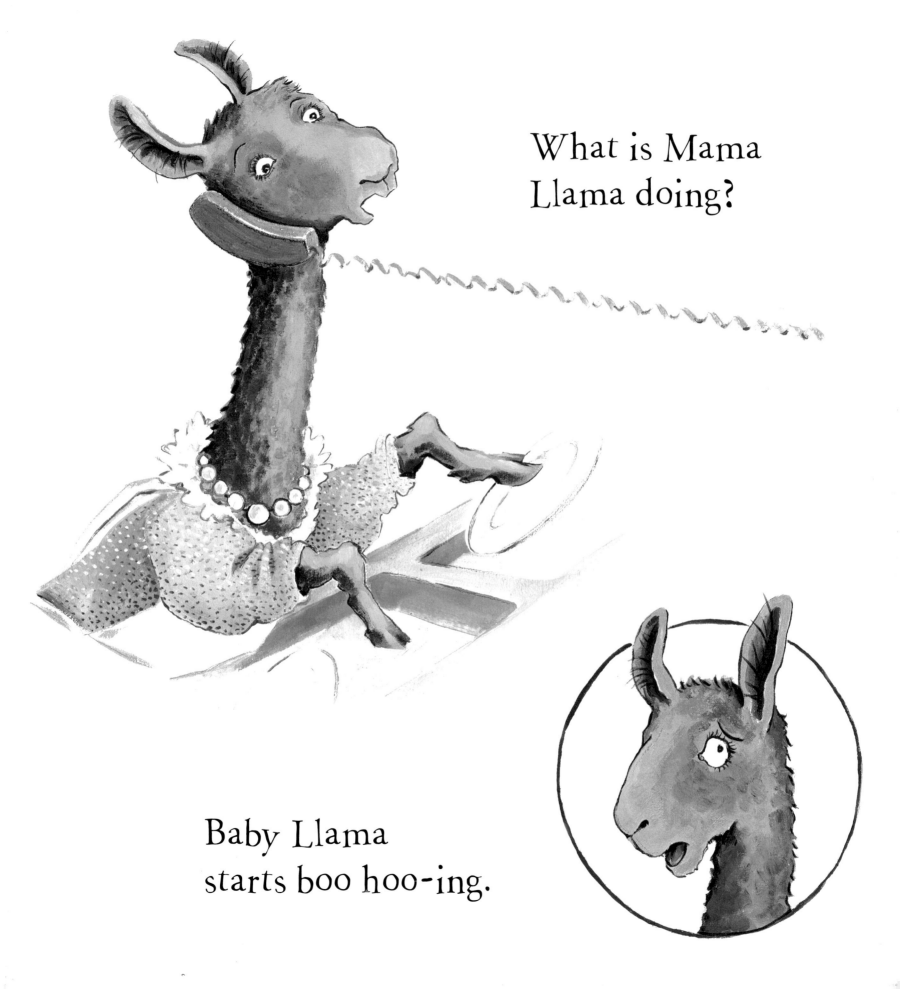

What is Mama
Llama doing?

Baby Llama
starts boo hoo-ing.

Llama llama red pyjama
hollers loudly
for his mama.

Baby Llama
stomps
and pouts.

Baby Llama
jumps
and shouts.

Llama llama
red pyjama
in the dark
without his mama.
Eyes wide open,
covers drawn…
What if Mama
Llama's GONE?

Llama llama red pyjama
weeping, wailing for his mama.
Will his mama ever come?
Mama Llama,

RUN RUN RUN!

Baby Llama, what a tizzy!
Sometimes Mama's
very busy.

Please stop all this llama drama
and be patient for your mama.

Little Llama, don't you know,
Mama Llama loves you so?

Mama Llama's
always near,
even if she's
not right here.

Llama llama red pyjama
gets two kisses from his mama,
snuggles pillow soft and deep...

...Baby Llama
goes to sleep.